Astronauts

Are Sleeping

by Natalie Standiford

illustrated by Allen Garns

Alfred A. Knopf
New York

Out in space, in darkness deep,
A silent silver spaceship gleams
And threads its way among the stars.

Three astronauts are fast asleep.

What are they seeing in their dreams?

Are they dreaming of the moon?

Round and glowing, pearly white,

It circles all around the Earth, like a runaway balloon held aloft by magic light.

Or are they dreaming of the stars—
Monstrous fires in blackest ink
Clustered into galaxies?

Do they dream of dusty Mars,

Where the sun sets blue and skies are pink?

Do they dream of airless Mercury? Or stormy Jupiter's Great Red Spot?

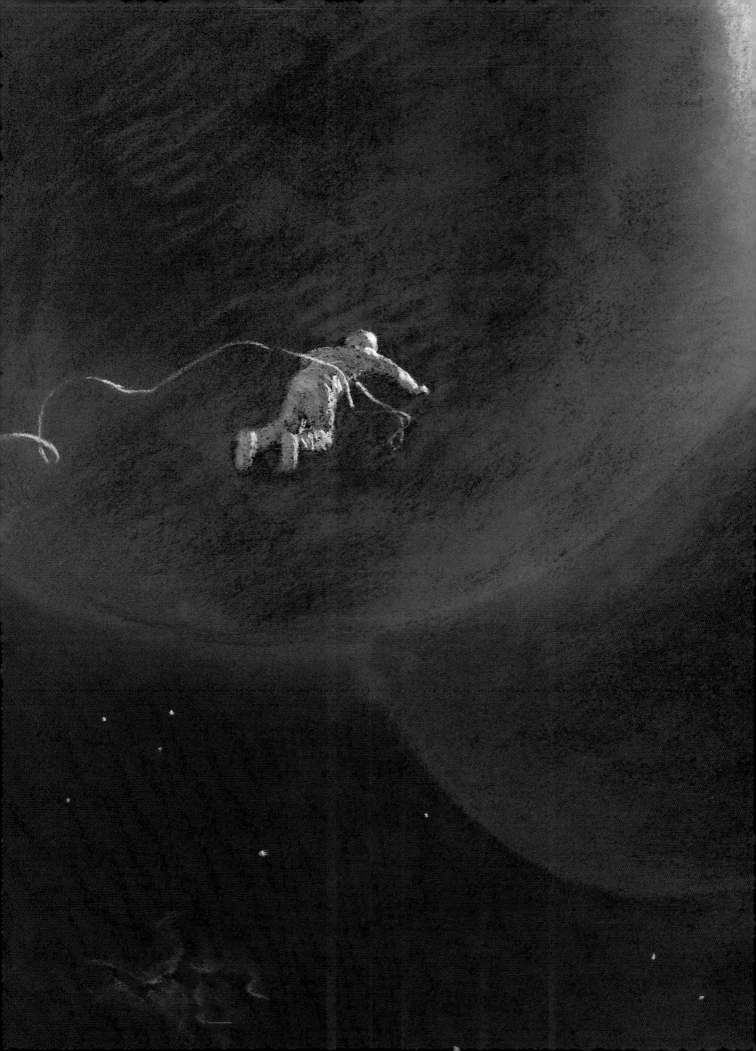

Uranus' halo of debris?

Neptune, like the blue-green sea?

Volcanic Venus, sizzling hot?

Do they dream of golden Saturn,

Rimmed with crackling, icy rings?

Do they dream of lonely Pluto?

Each whirling planet, in its pattern,
Spins and whizzes, hums and sings

The astronauts sleep soundly now.

Their weightless bodies tilt and bow

While wondrous sights go flashing by.

No dreams for them of nebulae,

The gassy clouds where stars are born.

No nightmares of black holes forlorn,

No Milky Way, its spiral beaming.

What
could
these
astronauts
be
dreaming?

Dreaming,

drifting back through space,

A time long past,

a distant place...

One dreams of sand between her toes,

The bracing chill of ocean sprays,

The taste of sea salt on her tongue.

The sun shines warm. A soft breeze blows.

She splashes in the waves to play.

One dreams of walking with his dog,

The warm rain dripping through the trees.

The misty woods are whispering.

The dog stops short, and through the fog,

A flash of red—a cardinal flees.

The third dreams of a winter's day:

Bread dough rising, smells of yeast,

A crackling fire perfumed with pine.

Outside the sky is metal gray.

A snowstorm blows in from the east.

They dream of sweet times long ago:

A glass of milk.

Turn out the light.

And sink into a soft, soft bed.

The moon shines on the sparkling snow.

Now kiss the one you love good night.

They're dreaming of the planet Earth.

The Earth's heart pulses like a drum.

The universe is vast and deep.

The stars burn bright with mystery.

The whirling planets spin and hum

And rock the astronauts to sleep.

For Craig
   —N.S.

For Ali, Paul, and Ben
   —A.G.

THIS IS A BORZOI BOOK PUBLISHED BY ALFRED A. KNOPF, INC.

Text copyright © 1996 by Natalie Standiford
Illustrations copyright © 1996 by Allen Garns

Library of Congress Cataloging-in-Publication Data
Standiford, Natalie.
Astronauts are sleeping / by Natalie Standiford ; illustrated by Allen Garns.
p. cm.
Summary: While spinning through space, three astronauts dream of life on earth.
ISBN 0-679-86999-9 (trade) — ISBN 0-679-96999-3 (lib. bdg.)
[1. Astronauts—Fiction. 2. Dreams—Fiction. 3. Stories in rhyme.]
I. Garns, Allen, ill.   II. Title.
PZ8.3.S786As   1996
[E]—dc20   94-37961

Printed in Singapore

10 9 8 7 6 5 4 3 2 1

First Edition